THE LARCH PLANTATION

A

. . . old Duncan, squat and muscular,
smelling of tar and fish,
and for thirty years obdurate
at the helm of his own skiff . . .

—'Bait-gathering'

THE
LARCH
PLANTATION

ANGUS MARTIN

LINES REVIEW EDITIONS

MACDONALD PUBLISHERS
EDINBURGH

8 2 /
M A R

F

ISBN 0 86334 069 5

Published in 1990 by
Macdonald Publishers
Loanhead, Midlothian EH20 9SY

*The publisher acknowledges
subsidy from the Scottish Arts Council
towards the publication of this volume*

Printed in Scotland by
Macdonald Lindsay Pindar plc
Edgefield Road, Loanhead, Midlothian EH20 9SY

Contents

Acknowledgements

Acknowledgements are due to the editors and publishers of *An Canan, Chapman, Lines Review, P.E.N. New Poetry I* and *The Scotsman* in which a number of the poems in this volume have previously appeared.

BAIT-GATHERING

for Maggie and Mary K

That was the coldest of mornings.
My father broke ice
on the pools of the shore,
waiting for ebb.
He had gone too early,
descending the foot-sculpted stairs,
down from his attic bedroom,
bearing no light that wintry morning,
a small boy dragging a wicker creel with him.

His father stirred him,
old Duncan, squat and muscular,
smelling of tar and fish,
and for thirty years obdurate
at the helm of his own skiff,
his pride as bright to the end
as superlative yacht varnish.
His hand, as hard as barnacles,
and longer tried by common elements,
touched his son who quivered in sleep,
some innocent dream alive in him.
'It's time,' was all he said.
My father woke, and time was in his mouth.
He dressed in the chill room,
and his shadow danced for him,
fantastic on a wall.

He broke ice and kicked at darkness.
His basket tipped on its side
and rocked on the bared ebb stones.
Soon he would pack it up with mussels,
with frozen hands unfastening them,
a child's tears filming his eyes,
that fisherman's son, torn from sleep,
as a living fish, in its shell of grace,
is riven from water.

7

GOAT

I laughed when the painter, Caroline,
delicately balanced on her nineteen years
assured me that poets were obsessed with death:
she hated my pictures of drowned cats.

Today, on a frozen mountainside,
her solemnity tunnelled out to me
from the seized brain of a carcase,
a goat once, prancing on the roof of the world.

What lives and moves disorders the universe.
A rock dislodged by a foraging goat
falls out of place and tries its weight in air.
It leaves behind a hole in the earth, a silent vacuity.

Death too is silence, and must detain the poet:
the end of his art is lodged in it.
So, I looked today on death, and looked on silence,
a goat that was in the world, yet knew no part of it.

Immobile on iced immobility of mountain,
it was itself its final alteration
of the eternally altering vastness
of moveable earth and stone.

GRANDFATHER

Grandfather's boat is out tonight.
The sea is galloping along beside her.
The sea has a simple sense of fun.
Nobody ever understood the sea.

He is an old man now, my grandfather.
Everybody thought that he was putrid.
Maybe he got restive underground.
He wanted a smoke and just got up.

The lights were strange around him,
but he sniffed the wind and came to.
He was seen determined on the trashy shore.
He was seen efficient at the fouled moorings.

The town woke up to the crack of a sail,
and grandfather was steering out beyond the living,
his whiskers probing the risky dark,
antennae of an indomitable patriarch.

They are in the storm together, boat and man,
ripping water on their final voyage.
My grandfather has no mind for herrings:
he scans the smoking runs of ocean.

He forgot that he had no future.
He raised himself and shambled,
in the roaring night of a world disordered,
to the mouth of the summoning sea.

He has gone, that exceptional corpse,
at peace on an unreturning tide,
out from the land that could not hold him
and the furious howl of his grave abandoned.

THREE HUNDRED GEESE

Three hundred geese got up
and shot their practised arrows
over the foraged fields
of Laggan late this evening.

This will be goodbye to geese,
goodbye.

They beat away on a wind of spring
and will forget that they were ever here,
that gaggling host

loud from the bow of instinct.

GRASS

That stalk of brittle mountain grass—
paled by the chilly suck of winter—
is caught in the carpet fibres yet.
If it had brains it wouldn't know
what to do with them.
Anyway, its root is stuck elsewhere
in a hard place for grass and all.
That stalk got here in someone's boot.
Grass seldom travels far except in the guts of animals.
Nobody seems to want to be kind to grass.

Last night, I swear, I heard the song of grass
here in this room, a song I'd heard before
one evening I was walking
with stones and sand in my pockets
and the cold stare of the moon
imperious over my left shoulder.

By the strayed effulgence of a dream
I looked about, and suddenly
I was walking far at sea
through roving meadows of the sunlight
shaking and hissing all the way to Antrim.

SHEEP

for Robert McInnes

Sheep is a bad imitation of some ancestor
that champed the herbage of a fresh world
before our species attained the talent
of whistling meaningfully to dogs.
But dogs were no better than animals then,
wild and disobedient, and quite unlike
the dogs that are padding around today,
dogs that have acquired the qualities
associated with the civilised condition.

The skulls of sheep are decorative in wild places
and appear to have capacious cavities
where the brain would have been.
Sheep are supposed to be totally stupid,
but no sheep ever admitted to that.
The truth is more alarming:
sheep are incomprehensible to us
and do not deserve to be judged.
Left to themselves on mountains
they will make their lives easy
unless they get into trouble and die.
They never asked to be clipped or dipped
or sectioned into bloody mutton.

The sheep moves ahead of the wind
because the wind is uncomfortable
and might bring rain or snow.
Its arse is always to the wind,
which must mean something.
Humans will walk regardless into every wind
because they're always going somewhere
very important.

DYKES

That dyke has been standing around a long time
without once having realised it is a dyke:
but ignorance is no embarrassment to dykes.

Dykes enjoy being noticed:
they have no other pleasure in the world.
Insects, weasels, the smallest birds—
and numerous other creatures
dykes wouldn't recognise by name—
have been noticing dykes
ever since dykes were invented
by the first people who wanted
to keep things in or out.
Nothing understands a dyke like weasels,
and they have a lot going for them
once they get inside a dyke.
Birds rear their delicate families in dykes,
and weasels certainly know that too.

Dykes never actually get bored.
They never think, as far as anybody knows,
but they do a lot of looking
in a stupid, determined way.

The birthplace of dykes is where they are
and always will be.
The graves of dykes are dykes themselves,
no longer willing to stand up
to the responsibility of being dykes.

ABORTED ELEGY
FOR GEORGE CAMPBELL HAY (1915-84)

Since the miserable death of my strange friend
I have wanted to write an elegy
that would not serve my vanity.
There was little vanity in that man:
his power and dignity raised him
above the petty scribbling talents
that would not recognise a poem
if it jumped and bit them in the arse.

Today is as good a day as any
to contemplate my friend and frame his worth.
The folly is that I must occupy this poem
as much as he, for whom it is composed.
If that is vanity then I swear
I'll drop my trousers when I recognise it
permitting any poem that Campbell Hay approved
to sink its teeth into my butt
until the blood of my Gaelic ancestors
spurts out in torrents.

Today I have been walking on the hills
of his Kintyre, but on hills he never knew
(he to the north, I to the south.)
I stopped to rest on the bank of a burn
and heard a voice that he too heard
on the Laggan hills before my birth:
comhradh an alltain—'the wee burn's talk.'
It told me that my friend was still alive.

If he was not here in his years of living,
he may be now, unless reality
is that hard thing I feared could not be broken;
and if he's here, the rain won't trouble
him as it troubles me: this page,
awash with drifting drizzle
from the vague and hazy hills west,

14

refuses any longer to receive
an elegy to any man,
least of all that man who may be here,
quiet at my shoulder in the trembling rushes,
and writing out, himself, his elegy
to make it tell.

I laugh, at last, aware at last
that his death was just a big mistake.
He does not need my elegy
and I do not need my vanity.
The rain has ended and the avid burn
brims with the chatter of its new waters,
and overhead the skylarks glance,
drenched but proclaiming irrepressibly
the living world that is endless to them
because they were not told of death.

TREE

The littlest of my interesting friends
broke my sleep on a rainy Sunday
to show me what he'd gouged from a hill:
a dangling tree, as big as himself,
clutched in an innocently soiled hand,
the earth of its ravaged roots
fast with unfiltered rain.

I complained of inexcusable destruction
of the nature that lies outside us,
but he would not understand,
wanting only a tree for his garden,
a genuine stick to gather birds.
He loves the birds and would do anything
to get the birds inside his vision.

I suppose he hasn't got to thinking
that trees could be loved as well.
He will not heed me, anyhow,
nor will he heed the captive tree
beating its dying head outside his door.

ENCAMPMENT AT THE INANS

for Judy

Sentiment—a grease on the mind.
I break the film and find your face beneath it.
Sun-flashings on the slack skin of the Atlantic;
moonlight filling a small tent—
you woke to it, but I slept on.

Between the stations of sun and moon
we walked together on the string of a bay,
the sea playing it, an old song.
We were in the two lights,
but which of us could make the choice:
sun or moon? Another light leapt on the shore,
a fire of driftwood gathered from
the legacy of winter's tides.

We sat on the blackest rock and watched
a light coming and a light going,
and the lesser light that would remain
for as long as we could give it force.

We left in the heat of the day after,
the sun a raging tyrant—inescapable—
and the moon as faded as an old dead moth
cold in the ash of a done fire.

AUNT

We quarrelled years ago about
inscriptions on a stone above a grave
that you no longer may attend
with flowers and a lugubrious hat;
but when I saw you lately
I could have cried with shame
that my wilful pride and pettiness
had kept me from your home.

You are a woman done,
and the world will soon be done of you:
white hair unwashed and stiffening
about a grey collapsing face,
and your body frail as an old stuffed heron
crumbling in the glass of a grim museum
that nobody cares to visit any more.

You cannot leave your bed now
and your smell has made the room
undoubtedly your very own.
I thought that I smelt death there,
but it may have been that guilt of mine
oozing from every pore of me
because I was remembering,
as I turned my back on you
and stood at a quiet familiar window,
that you were my father's sister.

You'll have a stone yourself soon,
above your quiet head,
and there will be no disputation:
who quarrels with the dead?

SPIDER

You have gone, spider,
but I shall replace you with a poem,
to prove that there is art in death.
How superior I am with my ideas!
I sent you, with a shock of water,
down the whirlpool of my kitchen sink.
I saw you there this morning,
brown and patient under
the sheer and slippery walls
of the trap you scuttled into.

I had twelve fresh and gleaming herrings
to wash and gut today;
into the sink I slid them
and turned a tap full on.
I saw you for an instant
floundering in the whirling water,
still brown and spidery, but
no longer patient.

The plug-hole was your grave
and into it you plunged without complaint.
Nobody regrets you, little spider,
not even I your literate killer.
I have my poem now;
you have your death.
Our interests met today,
and 'destiny' has a cruel sound.

19

RAVENS

On the last hills out west
where men and women live no more
and history is unforgiveness—
a creeping lichen gnawing stone—
bold ravens sit and wait for death.

Death is unending, and ravens know
that death is unending, so they sit
and wait on knuckled rock,
and the world is a stone inside their heads
with blood upon it.

Yet, ravens play at living too:
they spin in the languid air
or call in glad wind-tunnels,
but the earth is a stone beneath them,
with blood upon it.

GULL

Tall yellow flowers
hemmed the shore track,
an ailing gull within them,
head poised.

The air was close
and thunder muttered.
I sat on a rock
and filled my pipe.

Cattle came to watch me.
Flies worried them:
their ears flicked
and their tails beat.

The evening held on
and thunder grumbled
again and again
distantly along the hills.

That gull has followed me
to my house.
It is here with me,
impassive in this room.

It brings me, quietly,
its own extinction.
It mattered little
in the world.

Gull, with final grace,
could well have laid
the gift of its death
among the yellow flowers.

IN MEMORY OF HUGH MACFARLANE
OF TARBERT, DIED 3 JUNE 1979

I have been a long time, Hughie,
getting round to you,
but my faith was firm
as the blade of that old tobacco-knife
of yours, that your son laid by for me.
I keep it, but have never used it:
you were the last to pull the blade.

I'm sure that on the night
death entered you and broke you up
and blew your spirit into *cobharach,* *
you sat by the fire and sliced your plug
and filled your pipe and lit it
with a single steady flame and let it
concentrate your mind.

I put your years into a book,
your stories that were pressed
in glittering layers down shafts of memory.
I thought that I was mining
the last gold of my culture,
and feared the seam
would crack and crumble

before I had it delved.
That gold was endless,
and little dirt and dross with it.
I could be scooping at it still,
but death put up its fences
and its final closure signs
and that vital brain has gone to sludge.

You gave me more than stories.
You gave me the making and working and mending
of nets and lines, and the rigging of sails,
and the ways of herring and of the predators

on herring; you gave me the hard lives
of the skiff fishers, and you gave me
the old tongue from the mouths of the dead.

You have joined your old instructors.
How's the crack now, where you are?
Gey dreich, I'll wager!
No moonlight changing water where you are;
no wind to chase and scar the tides;
no silver of herring quick in the net's bunt;
no whisky streaming golden at the Corner House.

I'm back once more at Kingsway, Hughie,
and you're still there. I'm off the bus
from Campbeltown and seated on the low bench
at your kitchen table, forking breakfast.
You're quite at ease by a cracking fire,
puffing and thoughtful till I should join you,
your big moustache as bright as next year's snow.

* Gaelic, 'froth,' pronounced 'coarach'

TONIGHT THE FLEETS

Tonight the fleets are on the water.
Every boat that ever sailed
out to the fields of herring
cuts a burning furrow
in the living phosphorescence
of the powering ridges.
The fields are greeny water;
their crops are keen and glancing.

What are those voices
that thread the darkness?
The seabirds snap them
in the air, like thin wires
taut across centuries:
the Gaelic of the buried men
of Minard, Tarbert, Carradale,
and the guttural Scots of Campbeltown.

Their graves are opened up this night,
the rough-walled yards disgraced
by upheaved earth, and headstones
overthrown and shattered,
their lists of dead obliterated.
But no one saw the steady march
of cheerful bands to the old harbours
crammed by craft that had gone for kindling.

No one saw—no one remained
to see, and every light was out.
There was an end of culture, history,
and an end to the burial of dead.
How could those good men sleep on such a night?
Perhaps there will be herring caught again,
and nets hung up to dry, and weather watched . . .
but tonight they merely try their hands.

WOOD

Concerning the history of wood,
the sea has much to say
in its many vying voices.
But the sea is no judge of wood,
knowing only the broken ends of trees,
and trees have no notion of the sea—
their birth is small in earth;
their faith goes straight to the sun.

Wood may journey in its death only,
blind on the back of the ocean,
night and day through a hell of water.
Trees are noble, lonely things
that passion cannot touch.
Songbirds visit them with passion,
but the ocean birds look down on trees,
pitching far at sea, and pass.

All wood returns to land,
to rot in graves of sand or gravel
or stand grotesque in a waste of rocks,
lodged for the wind to warp and powder,
in death still monumentally
trees, but bare and birdless.
Hear out the history of sundered wood,
told in the mouth of the rootless sea.

FOREST

for Sid Gallagher

Since I lately came to live
in an old house with a fire in it,
wood has got into my vision.

I put my saw to wood
and glance a nick, and then I cut
wood into bits that please me.

Weight and form may please me,
and I am pleased to own
what at last I have to burn.

I am a Scottish wood-collector;
I belong to a great tradition
of bleeding hands and thick coats.

Wood accumulates about me;
I build it into piles,
I bag it and I lug it.

I love the look of wood:
its surfaces are maps and pictures,
and staring eyes and voiceless mouths.

Wood to the end is unresisting:
it lets me lift and drag it
far from the place that it lay down.

Wood will never fight
the blade's truncating stroke
or scream when fire consumes it.

But I had dreams of wood.
I was alone in a high forest,
sun and seasons banished.

The trees bent down their silent heads
and closed their branches round about
and I was gathered into air.

I burn in my dreams of wood,
a melting torch suspended
in the dark heart of a silent forest.

ORPHAN

You trail a dead lamb's coat,
sodden and shit-defiled,
through the mean and reedy grasses
of a wind-bitten field.

Your mother perished on the hill,
but through that winter's course
she carried you, then let you out;
you cried and hungered by her corpse.

Another lamb, that died at birth,
was skinned: you bear its scent
and at its mother's udder suck
credulous and content.

You draw the milk intended
to thicken another's breath,
and teeter meekly to survival
garbed in the weight of death.

MALCOLM MACKERRAL

MacKerral, that was one hard winter.
Your father died on the moor road,
his bag of meal buried under snows.
Death relieved him of his load.

Raking wilks with freezing fingers,
your little sisters crawled the shore,
scourged by gusting showers
until their knees were raw and sore.

Your few black cattle, thin and famished,
lay and died at the far end
of the draughty common dwelling.
There was little else you owned.

In the factor's oaken-panelled room
that the shafting sunlight glossed
you looked for your reflection:
you had become a ghost.

That month a stranger entered
the green cleft of the glen.
You watched him coming, from a hill,
and stabbed the earth again.

When he returned he brought the sheep.
At the house where you were born
you closed a door behind you.
Two hundred years had gone.

There was no end to the known land.
You looked, and there were names
on every shape around you.
The language had its homes.

Words had their lives in rivers;
they coursed them to the sea.
Words were great birds on mountains,
crying down on history.

Words were stones that waited
in the silence of the fields
for the voices of the people
whose tenures there had failed.

You knew those names, MacKerral;
your father placed them in your mouth
when language had no tragic power
and you ran in your youth.

You ran in the house of the word
and pressed your face upon the glass
and watched the mute processions
of your grave ancestors pass.

Look back on what you cannot alter.
Not a stone of it is yours to turn.
All that you leave with now:
lost words for the unborn.

MOUNTAIN ROADS

for Bob Smith

There are roads that no one travels
out on the spurned mountains.
The mountains are hard to the heart;
their memories are shed in streams
and are the food of dark-coloured fish,
stunted but proud
in the shade of leaning banks.
The eyes of the fish see a world
small and familiar to the last stone.

The mountains see nothing
and cannot celebrate their greatness.
Men marked the mountains:
ditched and drained and walled them,
dug the black and secret peat,
and bared their tracks.
Nobody went to the rock.
They stopped before the rock:
who would make a labour
hewing mountain
when all its broken
open faces lumped the fields,
a curse on tillage?

The roads are hiding now,
but under grass and bracken
the roads go wandering
lured by a moon that no one sees
rising big and calm
over the blue and silent
rise of mountains.
The moon makes its song
of stone to the stone
of the rooted mountains,
but the men are dead
who swung in the tide

of the evening's muted air
and through the waves of silence
heard the moon's
solemn song to sibling stone.

Yes, the roads go wandering,
like snakes on the sides of the mountains,
rippling air.
Where do they go?
They go where they have always gone,
to the places people laid
their mortal shadows on.
But the roads are lonely everywhere.
They pass the scattered stones
that stood for houses;
the fields that rocked with corn,
sunk in greedy rushes now;
the peat-banks that lay bare for yield,
mere pits of shadow now.

The roads are lonely in their journeys.
There was an end to voices
some time that is far
back in the time of roads,
and an end to feet
treading them, defining them.
A road without travellers
is a sad road,
but the roads have pride.
They wander by themselves
and meet where they have always met,
when the moon is a distant face
lighting up the empty lands.

PEAT

The mountains wear a dark flesh:
cold and damp and dead,
deep to the gravel lining bedrock,
and the great sculpted bone
of the mountain's being,
the essential mountain itself,
bulking rock rooted down
in the drifting rock of the world.

People toiled out there
on the sunny mountain flank.
They cut the flesh of the mountain
and fed it to their fires.
Their voices keep in brittle kernels
sunk in the silent peat pack,
like the barren nuts of hazel
that fell in an age of forests
and lay to the dour advance
of chill entombing bog.

Crack the shells and you will hear
a careless note of laughter
or a word or two from a wasted tongue
or the broken end of an old song
drifting from you.

EMPTY PLACES

Why do empty places trouble us?
Is it that the small
persistent intimations of mortality
wait out there to draw us?
A burnished fox that points its brush at nothing;
a wailing buzzard rounding on the wind;
a raven blackening a crag with waiting.

Is it that the people vanished?
Camp out there alone for days
attuned to wind and water only,
these tireless forces that attend
the greater motion of what men
still hesitate and call 'eternity,'
and you will hear the unexpected:
people's voices, tugged and torn
to scattered syllables, drifting on
beyond you in the bearing wind.

But are they 'real'?
I tell you, everything is real
out there, when you are stopped alone
on a broken ridge of jumbled stone
and the sky is the only traveller.

IN MEMORY OF JOHN CAMPBELL, DIED 27 JULY 1987

We've seen the last of the 'Snake Man.'
Hills and roads that knew his tread, mourn
for John MacFadyen Campbell
whose stomach filled with blood and bile.

I have it from a serpent's mouth
that John is happy in the earth;
his coffin is a little hole
that looks on neither heaven nor hell.

He frequented the snaky places—
rocks and dykes—and fixed his prizes
sure to the ground on a stick's
forked end, always able for their antics.

Vain prisoners, they would never eat
in the house of man, and he would let
them go when he was satisfied
with watching them. No serpent died

in Campbell's keeping. And when he was too old
to reach their haunts, he held
converse with the woodlice in his walls
and fed the birds and lifted snails

out of the path of heedless feet.
Now he has got the weight
of destiny upon him, that no one
may rise from under, and the known

sum of all his life is just
a sudden rumouring in trees, a lost
movement in the corner of an eye;
and he is quartered where the serpents lie.

PLACE-NAMES

I am the sole heir to maybe
a hundred place-names, snatched
from the cooling brains of farmers
and fishermen who have since fitted
neatly into holes dug for them
in a few places beginning with *Cill*.

To have moved among multitudes
of names, strewing hill and shore—
the bones of a great language
that perished in remoteness—
and to lie in death with a solitary name
tagged on the final place of all:

such is the narrowing of choice.

DALINTOBER

for my daughter, Sarah Campbell, b. 22.8.1987

There are evenings when I feel like walking round Dalintober,
usually when the light is gentle and patient,
encouraging the character of things to emerge.

The place is friendly to me,
like an old dog curled on the hearth of the loch.
But its tail never wags.
Its tail is the old stone quay,
and there is no life to move it
since the fishermen became extinct.

I used to meet the fishermen there
when I was drunk and rambling
in the dark after closing-time.
I wanted to meet them
and I suppose that's why
they dutifully appeared,
their intricately woven jerseys—
wrought on four needles, seamless—
so deep a blue that night
absorbed them. But I saw the faces
shining like new bone
or ivory, every feature hewn
out of the whiteness of the moon.

I recognised a few of them
from tired pictures. Some,
my ancestors, were kind to me,
spitting discreetly and opening
each his battered *spleuchan,* *
an offer I was always able to refuse.
They never spoke to me,
but stood apart,
their faces white and rapt
in helpless scrutiny.

37

I imagine now they puzzled
why I had brought them back.
Always they gazed around them
stiffly like statues waking
baffled on anchoring plinths.
They looked beyond the quay and saw
no skiffs at moorings, darkly
nodding their wearied prows,
hard wenches in a dream
of slain herrings.
They looked to the land and saw
impossible architecture
bulk where their homes had been.

They'd shuffle and turn their eyes from me,
uneasy with ancient debts
to times vacated,
and I would leave them then
to wander back alone
glimpsing heredity, small
in the eye of ruin:
sea-walls with mooring-rings intact;
the stumps of net-poles
rotting in the ebb;
boot-sculpted slabs descending into water;
street corners where they'd gather
in the lee of weather,
notching out an edge of stone
honing knives.

* local dialect, *tobacco-pouch*

THREE FOR SARAH

1

Why do you drop stones in the water?
You are my daughter and I have to know,
seeing I aid you in the matter.
Where do you think they go?

They go to the bottom of your mind,
I think, and stir some ancient sediment
of peaceful things that graced the sand
once, and that's why you're content

to drop stones in the water
day after day, somebody's daughter
a thousand years ago or more,
stooped and silent on the same shore.

2

You notice the smallest things in the world
that human eyes can see,
because you are very small yourself
and pay no mind to me.

I was intent on the big things
until you made me see
a bubble at risk on the ocean,
a leaf hanging on to a tree.

3

From whom did you learn to laugh so?
Not from me, I'm sure,
unless you caught some echo
of the child I am no more.

Your laughter lifts me like a cloud
gathering for rain;
I float in its pure suspension,
then fall to earth again.

PLACES

I get friendly towards places
that are kind to me—liberal
with sunlight, intolerant
of winds—and there is an inescapable

satisfaction in knowing
that the dead of my family
were also on good terms
with these enduring places, whose duty

appears to be the reception
of us brains-on-forks:
tramping about, excreting,
littering, and constantly releasing facts

and opinions that go up into the air
or maybe travel over the sea
like a host of winged insects
intense in their day.

HIBERNATION'S END

for Robin Fulton

Some creature may be curled asleep
under this tree that stands
with little to do all day but
fuss its many-fingered hands

or shake its head or push
a toe minutely further in
passivity of earth, nudging maybe
a tiny wintering bone.

FIELD HISTORY

And people lived here, humans
I tell you; children were born
and children died in this wet
hole in the rock; but a fire would burn

night and day, I suppose,
of wood thrown at their feet
by these same waves you see out there . . .
or ancestors of theirs, at any rate.

They ate from the sea, too—
imagine the ocean a great plate
feeding these prowling destitutes,
only it didn't put much fat

on them. A diet of *wilks*
and *gleshans* was hardly the ultimate
in rich living. Still, of those
that survived you couldn't have met

a hardier lot, I was assured
by old Bob Wylie who set creels
for crab and lobster
long ago down this shore. He calls

this place the Wee Man's Cove.
Notice the drystone wall
for breaking wind and rain
at the cave mouth, and sadly that's all

that remains of them, boys and girls,
unless we consider the hidden
end of all things material,
and that's it over there—the midden.

THE ENGINEER'S KIT-BAG

In the canvas bag were sundry clothes,
oiled and soiled and grimed with coal-dust,
clothes asleep, bunched *heids an thraws,* *
legs and arms entwined, at rest

in a throttled bag of darkness,
their bond the frame of a limited animal—
my father's frame, imprisoned on a boat,
going up and down inside compartments, his smell

and the smell of the loyal clothes
utterly the smell of compartments
in an old boat laden with coal
heading for places that made no sense

to a crouching boy with a map at his nose:
islands and sticking-out bits of the west,
the boat an invisible speck on the paper,
and his father an invisible speck on the first

speck, and the clothes on his father
invisible specks on the second speck,
and so on down to the specks
of dust and oil, of which I spoke

in the beginning, all miraculously returning,
shouldered ashore and home
by a seaman endlessly vowing
he'd quit the sea *this* time.

* *higgledy-piggledy*

43

ANCESTORS

All these people at my back,
watching me—out there—
people clothed in animal skins
and others only in body hair,

half animals themselves, poking me with sticks
in the soft parts of my unconscious,
startling me with sudden mad cries
and eliciting responses

that escape my knowledge
let alone my understanding.
I have been waking lately
in the middle of dreams, demanding

explanation, but they are secretive
and sly, and slide their sticks
under my bed and slink
along the walls, their shadowy backs

eluding me. But sometimes I will
lie awake and catch them unawares,
crouched in the middle of my room,
shielding small fires.

AIR

The air is blowing round and round the world.
It must be. I've breathed this air before
and will breathe it again if I've that long
to live, and can offer

my mouth to it.
Tonight it is blowing hard;
gates and loosened bits of buildings
clatter and bang, and I've heard

enough to start me thinking
of my father's life on the sea,
and how on nights like this
I would fear for his safety,

listening in bed with a small loneliness
lying beside me, breathing as I
breathed, in perfect unison, the air
that was serenity inside, and, outside, ferocity.

THE BIG OLD KEY

The big old key that rust is thinning
has lain in the glass-faced cabinet
at least since I was a prowling boy
and asked about it;

but nobody knew who'd owned it,
what lock it might have fitted,
in which door, where,
so it was fated

to become a thing obscure
and lost to history,
to shed itself in brittle flakes
till turned to nothing entirely.

LIMPETS

Limpets live in houses
which are portable,
but they never carry them far—
a foot and a bit, perhaps,
in any direction, grazing
the rock which is their sole domain,
a tenure unto death.

Limpets are mountain-dwellers,
abiding with their brothers of the rocks.
They have barbed tongues
and feed by rasping algae from the stone,
inching when the tide is on them;
but as it falls among the reefs—
cascading in weed-matted ravines—
they labour to the one place that is home:
a circle on the stone.

Then, when the rock is bared,
they must endure
sun and wind daily until death,
clamped in a perfect fit,
keeping their innards moist and functional.

When the rock is rough and hard they'll grind
the shell rim to its texture,
but given lease on sandstone
they must wear the very rock
to their circumference,
swivelling in the groove,
tide after tide, until intact.

And when death dissolves their grip
and their homes go clattering along the beach,
rolled in the wash of breakers,
the rings remain on the ebbing mountains,
inverted monuments no descendants seek.

HERE I AM

Here I am, watching the lower creatures.
I have nothing better to do,
my belly full and a wage
coming to me at the end of the week.

Ah, how wonderful to have
a highly developed intellect
and to be capable of understanding
the most intimate particulars
of their humble lives—particulars, I may add,
that they themselves will never understand.

Now, there's an eider on the tide edge.
Its arse is sticking out of the water,
therefore it must be feeding . . .

unless it too is watching lower creatures,
before it has to eat them.

LAMB

Back today at the Inans—
a kind of pilgrimage
to a loved and distant bay—
I walked straight into horror:
a plump lamb with the eyes
half-stabbed from his head.
Out, I thought at first,
seeing the arc of blood
he'd smeared around him on the grass,
casting his head from side to side.

I tried to raise him on his legs,
but he couldn't stand, and flopped again,
mutely writhing, bewildered and afraid.
I had intruded on
the manner of his dying,
but I couldn't let him be.
I held his head and looked:
the sockets were not robbed,
or not entirely, but blood congealing
masked the wounds.
I fetched him water in a dish
out of the gulley of Allt Dubh—
pure water from the mountain—
but he refused to drink.

And the sudden forms of hoodie
and black-backit gull
rose in my mind,
darkly on the brightness of that day,
and bitterness and hatred lay
under their veering shadows,
and I heard again the stabbing epithets
of farmers and hill-weathered shepherds
coming at me with a tired insistence,
turned aside and hollow till this day:
'vicious . . . wicked . . . evil . . .'

I could have dropped a boulder
on his head and ended there
the langour of his dying,
but his mother's face
was in my eye, enduring
all my fumblings with a mute reproach;
and I told myself the lie
that, after all, there might be hope:
he is not blind, he'll walk again.
The truth is that I could not end a life.

I kindled fire, supped tea
and ate, but the peaceful heart
of the day had turned
black in the clasp of my brooding.
I passed him on the journey out;
a last look, the one that shamed me.

Before the light has deepened
and the dipping of the sun
smears west with evanescent wounds
all will be, out there,
as it was before
I brought my burden of compassion
down through the glen of stones;
and the hoodies and black-backit gulls
will have his eyes
and steaming entrails,
and what remains
a fox by night will drag away.

—At Craigaig sheep-fanks, 3 June 1989

50

THE LARCH PLANTATION

for Teddy Lafferty

When the north wind forays
among the larches—
greener than all the greens assembled here—
I hear the sound of water boiling,
but really it's only the wind
stirring surfaces as the sun travels north.

SAINT CIARAN

for Fr Donald MacKinnon

In my cave I have seen Christ—
I the son of a poor carpenter—
and he showed me the tools
of my father's trade: plane and saw

in his hands that were smeared
with blood as though
he'd bled himself transforming
obstinate matter.

When Christ came to me
my back was to the rock.
I was watching daylight silver
the million sequins of the sea

and listening to the first birds tune
their pipes among the stones,
my mind as empty as a shell
turned on the farthest-reaching wave.

DANCERS

for Will Maclean

I am the boy who grew
like a limpet stuck to the quay.
I saw boats and fishermen
dancing on the sea.

And I wished that I could dance
in a yellow oilskin suit,
dance on the dancing water
to the slap of an old thigh-boot.

They were champions of some greater dance
performed in a night of islands;
o, show me your faces like grimy charts
and lay on my head your barnacled hands,

for I fear you have danced your passage
into the ports of the ground.
But I watch for your gull-haloed coming—
the limpet sticks around.

THE MAST

The horizontal—death to you.
When I saw you laid
in the muck and clutter of the quay
I knew that you were dead.

Not broken, split or flawed
that I could see, but unstepped
from mother deck and slung ashore
ungainly on a hook, you who leapt

at stars and rocked your head
over the surge of running seas,
or gentle on smooth sunlit waters
quietly nodded, upright and at ease.

Your grave is by the fish-shed,
under the lost, unmourning sky,
and only perching gulls will mind
your sea-years gone by.

I SAW SWIFT SAILS

I saw swift sails spectral on the water
and my spirit was restored,
on a wall-backed bench in wind and darkness,
without the intervention of a word.

How could they have called to me
or I to them, seeing that death unmade
their long voyage in the world
before my keel of bone was laid?

O, boats and men, when you return
to the scaly tomb of Dalintober
wordless as stone I'll meet you
in the dawn of the way things were.

AT POINT

A girl and a boy came to feed ten ewes.
He shouldered a bag of something loose
while her voice erupted echoingly,
commanding her charges: "Come and get it!"

These were the only people I saw today
here within broken walls, once home
to generations, dwelling where now
trees stand tilted like lengthening gravestones.

LOOKING FROM POINT TO BARASKOMEL

Now I look on places that I gave
days to, days that have blown
behind me like leaves from the rootless
tree of my life.

No longer there, I am no longer there,
but here, and what has become
of those selves that had belonging
in the time it took to cross

hill, shore, moor, anywhere?
I bear those times as growth-rings
in this mind that hangs above
the moving feet, a moon of white wood.

I HAVE REMARKABLE FAITH IN THE DEAD

I have remarkable faith in the dead,
that they may abandon their indolent ways,
rise and be useful, rise straight up in the world
like the blades of pocket-knives opening.

I have need of certain skills they possessed,
and an insatiable desire for instruction
in the cultural and linguistic attainments
that lay down with them and also became corpses.

BEN GULLION

for George McSporran

The mountain is always there,
giving itself daily to the eyes
as it stands with its fixed shrug
over the town, a benign giant.

I love it most when I cannot pay
its peace the homage of my feet,
in those evenings when the sun
coats its mass with mellow light.

But how different it is to walk on,
a hard god when weather turns,
and mist and snow—hostilities—
weigh on its real dimensions.

ISLANDS

Islands are bits of the land
that prefer their own company,
recluses that sea and wind
address in peculiar accents.

ERRADIL

for my daughter, Amelia Agnes, b. 11.8.1989

1

There is snow with the last of the sunlight
coming down through the neck of the glen,
and my pockets are heavy with shards
of china, each glaze-veined
with the dark earth's ageing.

Amelia, Amelia, Amelia MacKay—
I return your name to the stone-mounds
and the greening fields as smooth as plates,
feeding only sheep now.

I came here to speak your name,
you who broke through to the world
here, and grew to be a woman,
strong-limbed, industrious, beautiful;
and from the broken earth about the walls
I gathered these mementoes,
the spillage of ancestral middens.

Here is a curved, blue-patterned
rim fragment of a drinking bowl;
perhaps your young girl's lips were on that bowl
when some one called you from the fire
and startled you,
'Amelia! Amelia!'

2

I crave an intimacy with my great-great-great grandmother.
It is a perverse desire and will quickly pass.
I shouldn't be confessing any of this,
but today I sat by the shell of her birthplace,
a hill farm nobody speaks of any more:
night was closing in, and minimal snow salted the cold land.

61

I saw the houses rebuild themselves
and the roofs draw thatch from the rush thickets;
fires within sent plumes to their cloud-gods;
cattle lowed, and children bickered in shrill voices.

A woman came out and saw me sitting quietly.
She was lovely in her surprise and asked my name.
Her name, she said, was Amelia MacKay.
When I told her I came of her blood
and was folded in a dream out of my time,
she smiled and led me to a bed of straw.

3

Today I returned to Erradil,
drawn by a distant cloud of sails—
a ghost ship cresting hills, with its compass needle
tense and trembling on west.

It is the ship of the dead, and swings to an anchor now
on the smooth grazings where barley once
stirred in golden waves to the wind:
'The heaviest barley ever known to go into Campbeltown.'

The dead are wading through the green water—
laughing, glad, and all as one again—
to the rubble island that was home,
and a guiding light on the land swells.

Now I shall go, and leave them to their time,
fearing that I too shall become a ghost,
thinned to a spirit with my own kin,
but adrift still, beyond their recognition.

PAROCHIAL

I'm sorry, but I don't want to 'see the world.'
It's too big, and I'm content to remain
here on this sliver of its bulging
totality, discovering, today, a new tree
with a tape-recording of birds inside it;
tomorrow, a burn with the faces
of ancestors floating on it;
and the day after, a lost road—
in league with moss and heather—
that will end where I am.

DREAMS

Do I still travel or has
my passport been arrested?
'I'm sorry, sir, but the photo
doesn't fit your face.'

How long since I woke
at peace in the frame
of the coloured regions,
encased in foreign silences?

And what do I do with my nights
now? Are my dreams the turning
pages of a long dream-history,
at which I sit, in a room

with a small light shining on a table,
bare but for the book itself
and the dim moon of my face
on the veneer, the last dream?

64